A Taste of Blackberries

A Taste of Blackberries

Doris Buchanan Smith

Illustrations by Mike Wimmer

HarperTrophy
A Division of HarperCollins*Publishers*

Library of Congress Catalog Card Number: 88-45077
ISBN 0-690-80511-X
ISBN 0-690-80512-8 (lib. bdg.)
ISBN 0-06-440238-X (pbk.)

Published in hardcover by HarperCollins Publishers.
First Harper Trophy edition, 1988.

To Miss Pruitt
and others along the way

A Taste of Blackberries

Chapter 1

Jamie and I snagged our way into the thicket of the blackberry patch. I picked a dark berry and popped it into my mouth. The insides of my cheeks puckered.

"They need a few more days to ripen," I said.

Jamie had got stuck and had his thumb in his mouth. He took it out with a smacking sound and put his "shh" finger to his lips. Someone was coming.

"I'll bet Jamie and them will be sorry they didn't come," a voice said. I was "and them."

Jamie and I made faces at one another and pressed our lips together to keep quiet.

"Maybe they knew the berries weren't ripe," another voice said.

Jamie nodded. I almost laughed out loud.

"Well, that's what Jamie will say anyway." The voices began to fade. "He thinks he knows everything."

Jamie nodded again. He clasped his arms to himself, shaking in silent laughter.

"I've got to get out of here," he whispered. He started charging his way out of the brambles. The stickers snatched at him every which-a-way. When he cleared the patch, he fell down and rolled.

Jamie couldn't laugh without falling down in exaggeration. But he did have more sense than to fall in the middle of a blackberry patch.

I sat down cross-legged and watched. I could see the tops of the kids' heads as they went down the hill. It was funny, that we'd been right there, hidden, and heard them talking about us. But it wasn't worth having a fit over.

That Jamie. For my best friend he surely did aggravate me sometimes. I mean, if we got to pretending—circus dogs, for instance—he didn't know when to quit. You could get tired and want to do something else but that stupid Jamie would crawl around barking all afternoon. Sometimes it was funny. Sometimes it was just plain tiresome.

Jamie sat up, finally, and wiped the tears that had squeezed out from the corners of his eyes.

"Race you to the creek," he said. He hopped up and tore down the dirt road behind the houses. He had sneaked a head start on me and I really had to dig in to catch up with him.

If we started even I could always beat him. And, since he beat me in most things,

I wasn't giving him an inch if I could help it. I urged my legs into long strides and pumped my arms by my sides. I pulled ahead of him just as we reached the creek.

"Oh, you!" he scowled teasingly. He grabbed the side of my head and pulled me toward him, curved his leg around behind mine, then pushed.

As I went down I clutched his shirt and pulled him with me. We rolled around in the dirt until I said, "I give up."

Jamie would never quit, but I got tired after a while. I had seen Jamie fight with bigger boys. Even if he was getting beat, he wouldn't give up. If they let him go, he piled back into them, asking for more.

We rock-hopped the creek and sat down on the other side, where there was a fence to lean on.

Jamie's face was crimson. Dirt made streaks where it had stuck to the sweat.

"Is my face," I puffed, "as red as yours?"

He passed his hand across his face as though he could feel how red it was. He whooshed out his breath and leaned over the creek to splash his face.

"Brrr," he shivered. "That water must be about thirty-three degrees!"

I stuck my finger in the water to remind myself how cold it was. When we waded it was a challenge to see who could stand it longer. The water cooled the air around and the trees held the coolness under a green umbrella of leaves. You could even smell the cool.

Jamie finished splashing and nodded toward the other side of the fence.

"How about an apple?"

"Oh, no. Thank you," I said.

The fence guarded a farm that the city had surrounded. The farm was said to be guarded, also, by a farmer with a shotgun. Older boys made a game of snitching apples.

"Aw, come on," Jamie urged.

"Not me." I wrinkled my face and shook my head.

"Yeah," Jamie said scornfully. "You're afraid of him just like you're afraid of Mrs. Houser."

Mrs. Houser was Jamie's next-door neighbor, my across-the-street neighbor. Honestly, we tried to stay out of her yard. But if you accidentally stepped one foot inside her boundary line she shouted out her window. She seemed to be always looking out her window to see if anyone touched a blade of her precious grass.

"I don't think he would shoot a boy over an apple," Jamie said. "Come on, chicken." He started over the fence.

"Cluck, cluck, cluck," I said, trying not to let myself feel dared. "Chicken and proud of it." I grinned at Jamie, trying to joke him out of his idea.

Jamie up-and-overed the fence and started

across the field. My eyes skimmed the field until they bumped into the house. I thought I saw a movement at the door.

"Jamie, come back," I screamed.

Jamie kept going and never stopped. He reached the tree, shinnied up, grabbed a couple of apples, jumped down and started back.

The man had come out onto his porch. I fancied I saw a shotgun cradled in his arms. It was too far away for me to be sure. I ducked.

What would I do if Jamie got shot? Should I climb the fence and help him? How could I get him back over the fence? Maybe I should run for help instead.

I squeezed my eyes closed, waiting for the blast. Next thing I knew I was in the field myself, racing toward Jamie. He pushed an apple into my hand and we made tracks back to the creek. Two boys never cleared a fence so fast.

We skittered down the bank so we would be out of sight of the house.

"Did you see him?" I asked. My heart was beating paradiddles.

"Who? Him? Naw."

"He was standing on his porch watching you." Jamie raised his eyebrows with interest.

"He—" I could feel the corners of a square knot poking inside my throat "—had a gun."

I peeked over the bank. The day shimmered between golden sun and silver shade. Maybe there had never been a man, or a porch, or an apple tree.

But, there was the porch. There was the apple tree. And here was an apple in my hand.

"I told you he wouldn't shoot," Jamie said with false confidence.

I pushed the apple against my teeth and

broke the skin. Sour-sweetness spilled into my mouth. But my stomach was spinning faster than a playground merry-go-round and wouldn't slow down to let me swallow the juice. I spit and held the red fruit in front of Jamie.

"Want it?"

"Uh-uh," he grunted.

I tossed the apple and it landed with a plop in the creek. It showed white where I had taken a bite. I wondered if fish ate apples. I didn't want it to be wasted.

I glanced at Jamie. He seemed to be having trouble with his apple too, chewing each bit a little too long. I knew he would never admit it. He would eat it or else. I looked toward the water and stared at the apple, floating like a buoy.

When he had eaten his apple to the core, Jamie pitched the remains at my bobbing apple. His throw struck and the target tilted.

[9]

Jamie was a good shot, with an apple core or a baseball.

We followed the creek to where it curved at the paved road. I always hated to come away from the creek. One minute you were all secret and far-away feeling, and the next, here you were back in the world.

We trudged up the road, Jamie and I, not talking. Our feet made scuffing sounds on the pebble pavement. I struck my shoe against the surface. I felt if I did it hard enough I could make sparks.

"See ya," Jamie said as we came to his yard.

"Yeah," I said, not looking up. "See ya."

I took one last swipe at the street before I stepped into the grass of my yard. Someone called me. I turned around in time to see Jamie disappear into his house. There was no one else. I frowned. The call came again.

It was Mrs. Houser.

She was coming out of her house, calling me. I flipped my mind back a minute. Had Jamie and I walked on her grass? No. We had kept in the street even though a few feet of everyone's yard was really public property.

I felt like glass. Mrs. Houser could see through me. She could see Jamie scramble after those apples. I felt that I had done it, too. I wanted to run.

I swallowed hard and moved my feet toward her. She met me at the edge of the yard.

"Haven't I seen you children gathering Japanese beetles?" she asked.

Japanese beetles? What did Japanese beetles have to do with anything?

"Yes, Mrs. Houser," my voice took over.

"Well, I'm having problems with them on my grapevines and my yard man can't come. I was wondering if you could get some of the boys and girls to help me. I'll pay you a quarter a jarful."

Apples and jars and Japanese beetles whirred behind my eyeballs. I knew I could get the kids to help anyone else. But Mrs. Houser?

"I'll try," I said.

Chapter 2

First I went and told my mother. Then I went and told Jamie.

"Why should we do anything for her?" he asked. Which is exactly what I thought.

"I don't know." I ground the toe of my shoe into the floor.

"Now, Jamie, is that a nice way to talk?" That was Jamie's mother. She was holding Jamie's baby brother on her shoulder, burping him. Jamie also had a four-year-old sister, Martha. He was the oldest in his family. I was the youngest in mine, by far the youngest. My brother was married and my sister was in college.

"It's a job," I said. "She's going to pay us."

"Well, you know," Jamie got that far-away look in his eyes. "It might just be a lot of fun putting my feet all over Mrs. Houser's grass."

I laughed. It would be fun.

"And I bet every kid on the block will feel the same way," I said, smiling.

"Can we take Martha for a walk while we go around and ask the kids?" Jamie asked his mother. He really meant it. He didn't think of Martha as a pest, the way most brothers and sisters think of each other. Like my sister thought of me.

Of course, we went to Heather's first. Next to each other, Heather was our best friend. She tossed that golden hair of hers and said she'd love to help, just let her know when.

"Just as soon as we can go up the street and tell everybody," Jamie said.

"Just think," I said. "Being in Mrs. Houser's yard with permission!" She guarded her property as if every inch was a diamond mine. We didn't stomp around on her lawn. Really, we were very careful. But sometimes a ball or something would get out of control and roll onto her lawn. She screamed like a wild beast. She would threaten to call the police. Once she threw the ball at Heather. She missed by a mile and we couldn't help it, we laughed.

All the way to the top of the hill, our friends were interested in helping scrape Japanese beetles off Mrs. Houser's grapevines. Martha was excited too. We would have to let her help a little.

"I've never been so far," she said, looking down the hill toward her house. "Where is your school?"

"It's about two blocks that way." I pointed in the direction of school.

"Can I see it?"

"Sure," Jamie said. "Come on, let's show Martha our school." I looked down the hill, then at the sky.

"We don't have permission. Besides, it looks like it's going to rain."

"Oh, a summer shower. Come on. It's only two blocks, and Martha's never seen my school." He was so nice to Martha. I didn't exactly agree with going, but I went. I always had a hard time saying no to Jamie.

We didn't get a block before blackness blew in from nowhere. It was no summer shower. It was a summer storm. Jagged yellow lightning and booming thunder sent huge splats of rain down on our heads.

Martha began to wail.

"Let's get under a tree or something," I said.

Jamie frowned. "You know under a tree is the very worst place to be in a thunderstorm."

"I know," I said. "But we have to do

something." We were huddling Martha between us, and she didn't like it.

"You know, the safest place in a thunderstorm is in an automobile," Jamie said.

"Oh, sure." Jamie was great with impossible solutions. "Just snap your fingers and your chauffeur will appear."

Instead of snapping his fingers, he stuck out his thumb, hitchhiking. I thought he was kidding until the first car along stopped. The man in the car leaned across the seat and pushed open the passenger door.

"It's a little wet for walking, don't you think?" he asked.

"Yes, sir. Could you give us a ride home?" Jamie bigmouth asked. I bumped him in the rear with my knee.

"Do you know him?" I whispered.

"Naw," he replied casually. "Come on." He climbed in beside the driver and hoisted Martha to his knees. Swallowing hard, I climbed in behind them and closed the door.

"Where do you boys live?" the man asked. I was glad Jamie answered, because I was tongue-tied.

"What are you doing so far from home with such a little girl?" he asked.

"We were taking my little sister for a walk. We were going to show her the school."

"Don't you know better than to hitch rides? I could be a kidnapper, you know." My whole insides fell to my toes. I felt Jamie's knee pressing into mine. I could see the man holding us for ransom. Or killing me and Jamie and taking Martha.

"Here's the turn," Jamie said. His voice squeaked. I didn't breathe until the man slowed the car and began to turn. Then Jamie and I looked at each other and grinned. At the same time the sun burst through the clouds in streaks of angel wings.

"Right down here at the bottom of the hill," Jamie said. I looked surprised. I wasn't wanting to be let out of a strange car right in front of my house. Reading my mind, Jamie said, "Well, if someone sees us getting out up here it will look suspicious."

"Do me a favor, will you, boys?" the man said. "Don't hitch rides. The next person to stop for you might not be the father of one of your schoolmates." Jamie and I both shook our heads and said, "Yes, sir."

"Yes, sir," Martha mimicked, but she really didn't know what was going on. She was glad to have the ride. She had settled down as soon as she was out of the rain.

My mother was standing at the door staring. As we got out of the car she came down the walk with her hands on her hips.

"Who was that and where have you been?" She had the uncanniest ability to suspect things. It seemed she could see me with my thumb stuck out—and I hadn't even stuck out my thumb.

"We took Martha for a walk," Jamie said quickly. "And one of our schoolmates' father brought us home when the storm came." Jamie had a quick tongue; I was grateful for that.

"Un-huh," my mother sounded suspicious. "And what is this friend's name, may I ask?" I looked quickly at Jamie.

"Ed Chambers," he said, smooth as anything. "That was Mr. Chambers who brought us home." Ed Chambers' father would be surprised to know it.

"He was a nice man," Martha piped up with her tiny voice. "He took us home from the rain."

"Well, all right," Mother said. "I just wondered where you were during the storm." She headed toward the house, and Jamie and I rolled our eyes at each other.

We took Martha home and went next door to check the grapevines. We thought the rain would have chased the beetles away. But those beetles were waterproof and still clinging. Jamie ran around the neighborhood gathering the kids while I got the jars from Mrs. Houser.

Chapter 3

It was while we scraped Japanese beetles off of Mrs. Houser's grapevines that Jamie got stung. One minute we were all laughing at Jamie; the next he lay upon the ground like he was dying.

Most of us had been busy working. We held a jar to the underside of a leaf and scraped down across the top of the leaf with the jar lid.

"Easy, now, you'll bruise the leaves." Mrs. Houser had said that fifteen times already. We were glad when she finally went in and left us alone.

It was a great satisfaction to rescue a

whole leaf before it was laced with beetle bites.

Jamie was horsing around, as usual, and not doing his share. But it didn't matter. We were getting paid by the jarful. If he wanted to waste time poking around at a bee hole it was beetle money out of his own pocket.

"You better quit that." Heather frowned at Jamie as he shoved a slim willow limb down into the bee hole. "You'll get us all stung."

"Aw, you're even scared of a little old bee," Jamie teased. He pulled the stick out of the bee hole and nothing happened.

"You see? It's just a bunch of Heather-bees down there. They're too scared to come out."

Suddenly there was a grand humming noise, louder than you would've thought bees could make.

"Look out!" somebody yelled.

The bees came swarming up out of the hole in a ball of fury. Everyone ran but me; I stood stock still. Those bees went after the kids in arrow formation, just like in the cartoons. The kids were all screaming and yelling and running for home.

Except Jamie. He was already home, next door to Mrs. Houser, and he wanted to put on one of his dramatic shows for everyone. He screamed and gasped and fell on the ground.

Sometimes Jamie made me sick. I twisted the lid onto my beetle jar and put it down. With the apples and the hitchhiking, I'd had enough of Jamie for one day. I cut across Jamie's backyard to avoid the bees and went down the other side of the house and across the street to my house. I looked back and Jamie was still putting on his act, writhing on the ground.

"You might as well quit it, you brat," I said under my breath. "Nobody's even watching you."

I caught the screen door with my foot just in time to keep it from banging. "Go back and close the door quietly," I'd heard a million times this summer.

I went into the downstairs bath under the stairway. I splashed the sweat from my face and made a couple of swipes at the towel with my hands. Then I went into the kitchen.

"Can I have my Popsicle now?" I asked Mom.

"May I," she said automatically.

"Okay. May I?" She nodded and kept poking around in the dirt of one of her potted plants. She kept a supply of Popsicles in the freezer, and we were allowed one a day. I rummaged around for a banana one.

"Take it outside, in case it drips," she said.

I went out and sat on the back steps. I wasn't about to go out front and give Jamie an audience for his show.

I made sure my tongue was wet before I darted it out for a lick. Popsicles were so cold straight out of the freezer. If you weren't careful your tongue would stick, like your fingers sticking to the ice tray sometimes. It could pull the skin right off your tongue, and nothing tasted right for days.

I got one little spot wet enough to start licking. The freezing coldness slid down my throat, through my stomach and clear to my toes.

I looked across our backyard to Mrs. Mullins' and wondered what she did about Japanese beetles. She probably grew grapevines especially for them.

Mrs. Mullins' backyard was like the secret garden. At first glance it looked like an overgrown jungle. The entire yard was planted in flowers, trees and shrubs with only paths in between. It was her wilderness, her bird sanctuary.

Even from here I could see different colored butterflies waving their wings amidst the growth. I knew that if I walked over to the fence and stood very still I would probably see a hummingbird.

I felt a little secret pleasure. I was one of the few kids who had ever been allowed into Mrs. Mullins' garden. All my friends thought she was a little weird. My mother was friends with her, and I had found out she was nice. She just didn't want a bunch of whooping and hollering kids to chase off her birds. At least she wasn't as grouchy as Mrs. Houser.

I held the Popsicle up and let the last bit slide off the stick into my mouth. I sighed. I was pretty tired of scraping Japanese beetles, but I knew I'd better go finish. If my father found out I had agreed to do the job and left so much as a single beetle, well.

I lifted the lid of the garbage can and dropped in the Popsicle paper and sticks. Then I went around the house, feeling very noble about not going through and slamming the doors.

As I came up front I saw Heather standing in Jamie's yard. She must be ready to start to work again, too. In the distance I heard a siren wail and cocked my ear to decide if it was the police, a fire engine or an ambulance. Some of the kids claimed they could tell, but I couldn't, unless it was one of the ambulances that shrieked whoop-whoop-whoop.

"It's Jamie," Heather whispered to me when I crossed the street. She lived next to Jamie on the opposite side from Mrs. Houser.

"What?" I squinted my eye and twisted

the corner of my mouth as if that would help me hear better.

"Jamie. Something's wrong with Jamie. I bet that's the ambulance coming for him."

"Aww," I said scornfully. What could have happened to Jamie so fast, unless he broke his neck in his falling down act.

The sound of the siren came closer and Mrs. Houser poked her head out of Jamie's front door.

I guess that froze me. Mrs. Houser never went to anyone's house around here. Heather and I didn't move or say a word while the ambulance came nearer.

Children popped out of doors and out of backyards to listen and watch. From the top of the hill the ambulance came, shining in the sun. The whole neighborhood flowed down the hill like water behind a moving dam.

"It's Jamie," Heather whispered as the yard began to fill.

The ambulance attendants bustled out of the side doors, grabbed the stretcher from the back and ran toward the house. In a minute they were back.

Sure enough, it was Jamie, lying still and pale, with his eyes closed. His mother was even paler. She piled into the back with one of the attendants. The other man hopped into the driver's seat and they sped off with a wail. Mrs. Houser stood in the doorway and everyone was quiet.

"What's the matter?" a voice broke the silence.

"All I know is he got stung."

"Stung? Huh! Look at me. I got stung eleven times!" The speaker began to point to his various swollen spots smeared with soda paste.

"Is he dead?"

"Don't be crazy," I said. "Nobody dies of bee stings." The awe in which I held

Jamie due to his emergency and ambulance ride suddenly burst.

"Likely he hurt himself having a fit!" I said. I went to Mrs. Houser's and picked up my beetle jar.

In just the few minutes I had been gone the beetles had multiplied and recovered every inch we had taken. Disgustedly, I began scraping again. I cheered up as the jar filled quickly. If the other kids were too lazy to come finish I could really earn a lot of money.

The kids moved from Jamie's front yard over toward me.

"Where did the bees come from?" asked someone who hadn't been there. Heather tried to find the bee hole and couldn't, so I showed them. I picked up the stick Jamie had used for poking and pointed with it.

"See," I said. "The stick must have knocked dirt down inside." The bees were busy crawling down the hole and out again with dirt daubs in their mouths.

"Do you really think he's dead?"

"Don't be dumb."

"Boy, did you see how fast they ran in and got him?"

"I sure would like to ride in an ambulance."

"Jamie didn't seem to be enjoying it too much."

"Something sure is wrong."

"But, it don't have nothing to do with bees, whatever it is."

"Why don't we ask Mrs. Houser?"

"You ask Mrs. Houser."

They faded away and left me with the beetles, and I kept scraping. I knew if they found out anything, they'd let me know.

I heard the bang of a screen door and looked up. It was Mom coming across from our yard.

Hey, Mom. Go back and close the door quietly, I thought with pleasure.

She saw me looking and motioned to me as she came across toward Jamie's. I sensed her urgency.

By the time I screwed on the lid to the beetle jar and ran around front she was up to Jamie's door. I followed her in.

Chapter 4

Mrs. Houser was holding Jamie's baby brother, and Martha sat on the floor with a coloring book and crayons. Everything was dark and cool. Jamie's mother said the house was cooler if it was closed up.

"I'll take the children," Mom said to Mrs. Houser. Mrs. Houser handed over the baby.

"Son, help Martha gather up her crayons and take her over to our playroom."

"Jamie got stung," Martha said, barely looking up from her coloring. I reached under her armpits and pulled her to her feet. We left Mom and Mrs. Houser talking in hushed tones.

Martha dropped her crayons in the middle of the yard and we both stooped over to pick them up. I stuffed as many as I could into my pockets.

"That's the color of the am-blance," Martha said, holding the white crayon. "Did you see it? Did you see Jamie get a ride?" Her eyes were bright and excited. We were almost at the spot where the ambulance had parked.

"Yeah," I grunted. I guess I was the only kid in the neighborhood who hadn't been impressed by that ambulance. The whole neighborhood was running and squealing to see what was the matter.

That Jamie. He was an expert attention getter, even when, maybe, he didn't intend to be. I wondered briefly if he had been faking unconsciousness just to keep from grinning at all of us. It would serve him right if he was out cold and didn't even know he was riding in an ambulance.

Something in my conscience kicked me.

What if something really was badly wrong. Naw, it couldn't be. What could happen to Jamie the great? He yelled a lot, but he was tough.

If we were wrestling, he would scream sometimes so I thought I had really hurt him, but he would never give up, never. And he would do such crazy comic falls that you'd wonder how he kept from breaking his neck. Jamie was a show-off and a clown all right, there was no doubt about that. And most of the time it was funny.

I stretched out on the playroom floor and colored a picture for Martha. She could color pretty good for four. She didn't stay inside the lines very well, but the colors she used looked good together. I mean, she didn't dress a lady in black and purple. I colored my entire picture in shades of green, and Martha was very impressed.

Mother came in with the baby, and I stayed on the floor and started another picture. Part of me wanted to find out all about Jamie; but the other part was afraid to hear.

She lay the baby on the sofa and pushed a chair against it. The baby was asleep, all roses and cream. If I could put that color into a crayon it would be a miracle.

When Mom had the baby settled she called softly for me to come with her. She sat down at the kitchen table and motioned for me to sit down. I couldn't sit. Some awful instinct was hammering on my brain. I tried not to listen.

"Jamie is dead, darling," she said.

"Dead darling" rang in my head. Jamie is dead, darling. Jamie is a dead darling. He didn't look so darling flopping around on the ground, showing off. Jamie was a freak.

"I know," I said bluntly. "I saw the ambulance." I felt trapped. I didn't want to listen to her telling me lies about Jamie.

"Were you out there when it happened?"

[39]

"Yes."

"What happened?"

"Jamie poked a stick down a bee hole."

"Did you get stung?"

"No. I stood still."

"Then what happened?"

"Everybody ran."

"Did Jamie run?"

It was as though she had punched me in the stomach. I saw Jamie again, falling down and writhing. I closed my eyes. I shouldn't have left. I should have helped him. But how could I know? I swallowed. I thought I was going to be sick.

"Did Jamie run?" she repeated.

"No," I said. "He fell down. I thought he was faking."

She reached out to touch me, but I was out of reach and didn't move closer.

"I know," she said. "We all know how Jamie was."

My mind buzzed like that swarm of bees.

I hadn't even got stung, and Jamie was dead. Someone had got stung eleven times and it was just like giant mosquito bites, and Jamie was dead.

"How many times was he stung?" I asked. He must have been stung a hundred times.

"Just once or twice. It wasn't the number of stings, it was that Jamie was allergic to them. A few people are allergic to bee stings."

Allergic? I knew about that. A girl at school was allergic to chocolate. It made her sick. We all felt sorry for her. But I didn't know that being allergic could kill you.

"Did Jamie know he was allergic to bee stings?"

"No, he didn't, sweetheart. No one did. He wouldn't have played around a bee hole if he had. It was a freak accident. It hardly ever happens."

"How did they—? Who found him?"

[41]

"Mrs. Houser. She looked out to see if you were all working and she saw Jamie on the ground. She ran over and got Jamie's mother."

Mrs. Houser! I would have thought she'd just let you lie there and rot.

"I'm going upstairs," I announced. I went to my room and stood by the window, staring out. Did the world know that Jamie was dead? The sky didn't act like it. It was a blue sky and white cloud day. Horses and lambs and floppy-eared dogs chased across the sky. Was Jamie playing with them?

What kinds of things could you do when you were dead? Or was dead just plain dead and that's all?

I looked across at Jamie's window. He would never flash me a signal again. We had learned Morse code, Jamie and I, and talked to each other at night. Before that we had taken cans and a string and stretched it across from his window to mine.

That had been a funny day. It had been so easy to string up one can and drop the string down from Jamie's window. It wasn't so easy getting the string up to my window.

We dragged the string across the street and Jamie tried to throw the can up to me. I was a little scornful of Jamie's pitching arm until I tried it myself with him upstairs trying to catch.

Finally, I climbed my mother's rose trellis by the kitchen window, careful to keep my foot at the cross pieces of the trellis where it was strongest. I picked my way up through the thorns until I was on the sun deck with the can and string.

"Yeah, smarty," Jamie laughed. "Now, how are you going to get it to your room?"

We felt like engineers trying to set up a

communications system, but we figured it out. Then the dumb thing didn't work! We just flopped down exhausted.

"And you know what I just thought of?" Jamie asked when he came back over. "Why didn't we just drop an extra piece of string from your front window and tie onto this one and pull it up?" It was so simple we collapsed again and clapped our arms over our heads. We felt so stupid.

Later, we had got the encyclopedia and looked up Morse code. We saved our money and bought flashlights with blinker buttons. It certainly was easier than that stupid set of cans. And it worked.

So, my mother had told me that Jamie was dead. No more blinks from across the street at night. No more Jamie. Who would we have to make us laugh anymore?

Chapter 5

I sat in the bathtub and poked ripples in the water. Soapy whiskers covered my chin. I hadn't eaten lunch before and now hadn't eaten supper. Dad and Mom were getting ready to go to the funeral parlor. They asked me if I wanted to go, but I couldn't do that to Jamie. It seemed that as long as I acted like he wasn't dead, he wouldn't be dead.

The ring of ripples broadened, bounced off the sides of the tub and, larger still, came toward me again. Someone said that ripples go on forever and ever, even when you can't see them anymore.

I thought of me and Jamie throwing stones

in a still pond, watching ripples. Jamie wouldn't make ripples anymore. Or shampoo beards.

I grabbed the soap and rubbed up a lather. The soap was my lamp and I was Aladdin. I would rub life back for Jamie. Someone knocked at the door.

"We're going now, sweetheart. We won't be long. If you need anything, you go over to Mrs. Mullins'."

They were going. They were going to see Jamie. Suddenly, panicky, I yelled.

"Wait. Wait for me." I submerged and let the soap rinse off me. I rubbed my hair as dry as I could and combed it. Mom straightened my part. Usually my hair just hung there, but when it was wet it looked better combed.

I had never been to a funeral parlor before. I had been to a funeral, at a church, when my dad's Uncle Jonah died. He had tripped with his shotgun and blown off the top of his head. At least that's what they said.

The casket was open during the funeral, and row by row, everyone went by to look. As I went by the casket, I was prepared not to take a good look. But in just a glance I saw Uncle Jonah's whole head. Then I looked.

He was fixed up just like nothing had happened. He didn't look like he'd been shot. He looked like he was going to wake up any minute and ask us what we were doing, staring at him while he slept.

Of course, nothing like that had happened to Jamie. He had got stung by a couple of bees. It just didn't seem possible that a tiny thing like a bee could kill you. I guess a lot of bees were dead too, if it was true they died when they stung you. I wasn't glad the bees were dead. I was sorry about anything being dead. Especially Jamie.

When I had popped out of the bathtub and said, "Wait for me," I hadn't known why. Now I did. I wasn't going to look at him, but if it was possible that Jamie knew what was going on, I wanted him to know that I was here, thinking about him.

There were people all around, talking in whispers, or not talking. Some were crying. I leaned my back against the door frame, thinking to Jamie.

I'm here. I'm here, Jamie.

"He looks sweet," a woman said as she came out of the room. "Just like he's asleep, bless his heart."

I remembered how Uncle Jonah looked like he was sleeping. I couldn't imagine Jamie looking like that. I went in and pushed up between my mother and father.

There was Jamie. He was out straight with one hand crossed over his chest. He didn't look like he was asleep to me. Jamie slept all bunched up. Jamie looked dead.

We used to have these staring contests, Jamie and I. We would see who would blink first, or laugh.

It began to sink in that Jamie wasn't going to open his eyes to stare back at me. He wasn't going to blink. He wasn't going to laugh. I ran out of the room and down the hall.

The front yard of the funeral parlor was all green grass and colorful flowers, with lights shining on them. I snatched a yellow bloom from the stem and began tearing it to shreds.

My father called to me and grabbed my shoulder and turned me around.

"Daddy!"

I buried my head into his chest until the buttons on his suit hurt my face.

At home I put on my pajamas. Mother hung around, telling me that sometimes we don't understand why certain things happen. She waited for me to talk. I just lay

in bed with my hands behind my head. Finally, she touched my hair and kissed my cheek and left.

I listened to her steps disappear. Then I got up and knelt by the front window. There was my flashlight, in its place on the windowsill. Jamie's was probably on his sill too.

I flicked on my light and shined it over toward Jamie's to see if I could see his flashlight. Of course I couldn't. The beam didn't carry that far. When we signaled we could never see each other, only the dots of light. Unless we put the light up under our chins to make spooky faces.

There was the soft padding of footsteps in the hall, and I set my flash down and sprang into bed. They were coming to check. Every night Mother or Dad, or sometimes both, would come check to see if I was asleep.

I pulled the sheet up and scurried around

under it to find a comfortable position. I let my head flop down, tilted a little sideways. I raised my arm and tucked my hand along by my cheek. I took a deep breath and let out a big sleepy sigh. I almost convinced myself I was asleep.

The door made the slightest squeak as it opened. I imagined the crack of light slicing across the room. I didn't hear a footstep, but something touched my forehead. I almost jumped. I concentrated on keeping my eyeballs from moving around behind my lids.

It must have been my mother. The hand, touching first my head then my cheek, felt soft and smooth. She tucked the sheet up around my shoulders and under my chin, a habit she had even in the summer.

She stopped tucking, and I heard the door close.

I opened my eyes. Everything was so black, I wondered if she was still in the room, watching me. In a minute, my eyes were used to the dark and I could see she wasn't. I went back to the window.

The front door sounded below me. I didn't look down, I kept staring at Jamie's house. I saw my mother going through Jamie's yard to the door.

The sight of her turned on my tear faucets so suddenly that I was surprised. All day I hadn't cried, even when I pressed my face into my father's coat buttons. The strange thing is, I wasn't crying for Jamie, I was crying for me.

I wanted my mother to come back. I wanted her to take care of me. I wished I hadn't pretended to be asleep; then she would have stayed to talk or just to sit quietly on the side of the bed. I wished I was little and could sit on her lap and be rocked.

The tears kept coming until I had them smeared all over my face. My face was tight where the tears had dried. I was snuffling and fumbling around in the dark for a tissue.

The door opened again and Dad's shadowy form filled most of the crack of light. Out of habit I dove for the bed.

He came over and picked me up as easily as if I were a baby. He sat me on his lap and cradled my head to his chest. Funny, I hadn't thought of Dad's lap, but it was just as good. I cried and cried and cried.

Chapter 6

The next morning some of the kids were playing. I watched them out my window. They were playing "May I," but in hushed tones, because of Jamie. I wondered how they could play at all. The heaviness of Jamie's death was on me.

My father had gone to work, but he was coming home in the afternoon to take us to the funeral. All of Jamie's friends would be there. A preacher or someone would say some things about Jamie. Then Jamie would be buried.

I stood at the top of the stairway and listened for sounds of my mother. I heard the buzz of the vacuum cleaner. I tiptoed

[55]

down the stairs, slipped through the kitchen and went out.

I looked over at Mrs. Mullins' garden. Right now I wanted to be there more than anything. It was the most private place I knew. But Mrs. Mullins wasn't in the yard.

When Mrs. Mullins is in the yard sometimes we talk over the fence. Then she invites me into her garden and tells me all about growing things. But she wasn't there this morning, and I hated to bother her by ringing her doorbell.

Timidly, I went to the side gate, lifted the latch and went in. Once in, I wished I was out. I felt like a thief, stealing into her garden. I walked quickly down the nearest path, paying no attention even when a butterfly brushed my cheek as he flitted by. At the end of the path I looked back. I was out of sight of Mrs. Mullins' windows.

I sat down on a large stone. Granite, Mrs. Mullins had said it was. At first glance it looked gray, but if you looked closely it was speckledy black and white. Along one side there were streaks of pink and green.

The garden was radiant with summertime. My nose smelled the sweetness. I could almost hear the colors in my ears.

Every color seemed to be there. I looked around to see if there really was. There were all shades of green, from a pale yellow-green to nearly black.

There were yellows from pale to golden orange and oranges to rust brown; pinks, to reds, to purples. There were not many blues. My favorite of all was the bright blue raggedy cornflower.

I felt sorry about the flower I tore up last night. It wasn't the flower's fault. I breathed deeply and heaved a sigh.

Butterflies darted from flower to flower,

and bees. I didn't mind about the bees. It wasn't their fault either. They didn't know Jamie was allergic.

And there was a hummingbird, hovering like a helicopter then zooming away so fast my eye could hardly follow.

Only the sunflowers hung their heads, as if they were sorry that Jamie was dead. But they weren't sorry either, really. They didn't even know. They only hung their heads because the bloom was too heavy to stand up straight on the end of the stem.

A different sound reached my ear, and I glanced sideways by my arm without moving my head. Mrs. Mullins was moving slowly down the row of flowers. I could only see the feet and the bottom part of the person, but I knew it was Mrs. Mullins. No one else wore such raggedy tennis shoes and baggy britches. I hoped she wouldn't be mad because I was in her garden.

"Hello," she said softly. Mrs. Mullins

always spoke softly. Sometimes it was hard to hear what she said.

She sat herself down on a nearby stone. All around her garden she had stones, or concrete block and board benches—"So I can sit and look from wherever I want," she had told me once.

Her being there made me feel like I shouldn't have come. I didn't know what to say to her. The silence made me uncomfortable. Mrs. Mullins was a great one for not talking sometimes. The air felt empty; I had to say something.

"I hope you're not mad," I said. I didn't look at her. I stared at the ground between my feet.

"Mad? Why should I be mad?"

A question for a question. I didn't like for people to do that to me. Didn't she know why I thought she might be angry?

"Because I— You didn't know I was here."

"I saw you come in."

"You did?" I guess I expected she would have hollered out her window like Mrs. Houser— "Get out of my yard!"

"I was in the kitchen. You came in right under my window."

"You know about Jamie?"

"Yes. I am so sorry about Jamie. And sorry about you, too, because you were his friend." Mrs. Mullins was as gentle as the butterflies. They were so fragile looking, yet they could fly, some of them, like the monarch, for thousands of miles. Mrs. Mullins had told me all about butterflies.

"Why did he have to die?" The question lay there in the air between us. The sound of it shocked me, but Mrs. Mullins didn't act surprised.

"Honey, one of the hardest things we

[61]

have to learn is that some questions do not have answers." I nodded. This made more sense than if she tried to tell me some junk about God needing angels.

We just sat for a few minutes. This time the air didn't need to be filled. I let my eyes wander around again to the grass, the flowers, the birds—everything was alive. I was alive. Mrs. Mullins was alive.

"What's it like to be dead? Or is that another one of those questions?"

"It's one of those questions," she said. "You just don't know until you can find out yourself, and apparently you can't come back and tell what you find out."

"Jamie was special," I said.

"I know." Mrs. Mullins stood up and walked away. I didn't know if she was somewhere in the garden or if she had gone back into the house. I knew she meant for me to stay as long as I wanted. I stayed until my mother called me for lunch.

My sister was there from camp. She was a counselor. She had come home for the funeral. My sister and my mother were chattering with each other, catching up on the news.

They stopped talking when I came. My sister didn't say anything to me about Jamie, and I didn't say anything to her about him either. Maybe she was afraid I would cry.

I sat down at the table and put my hands in my lap. It was required at our house that you come to meals, even if you weren't eating. I hadn't eaten anything since Jamie died. The Popsicle was the last. It was over twenty-four hours now. My stomach was gnawing on itself. I had to force my hands to stay in my lap. My stomach was trying to command my hands to grab some food.

"Sweetie, it won't help Jamie if you make yourself sick," my mother said.

How could I explain to her? Maybe it didn't make much sense, but I knew I couldn't eat until after the funeral. Everyone was talking, eating, moving—just like things were the same. Somehow I couldn't let things be the same.

Chapter 7

Ever since it happened there had been cars parked all up and down in front of Jamie's house. They spread in front of our house and in front of Heather's and Mrs. Houser's. Mother kept running back and forth with pots of food, or bringing Martha and the baby over, or taking them back.

Martha talked to me about Jamie.

"Jamie's dead," she said. "Like that baby bird you and Jamie found and tried to feed but he died anyway. Jamie's not coming home again. Not never." Her little face still had a pudgy baby look, and she didn't cry at all as she talked about it. She might as well have reached inside me and snatched out some of my guts.

"He's in heaben," she said. "He's going to get to play with all the angels." She seemed happy for him.

When it was time for Martha to go back home, my mother asked if I wanted to go over with her. But I didn't. There would be people crying all over the place, and I wouldn't know what to do or what to say. Besides, it didn't seem fair to remind Jamie's mother that I was alive.

I did wish I could tell her that I would be her substitute son. I would help take care of Martha and run errands for her like Jamie did. But how could I tell her? Words were going around in my head, but they wouldn't come out of my mouth.

I went upstairs and ran water in the bathtub. I soaked until my fingers wrinkled. I kept feeling that if I did certain things, like think about Jamie in the bathtub, or didn't do certain things, like eat, that somehow everything would be all right and it wouldn't be true that Jamie was dead. Like it was really a dream and we would all wake up any minute, and there would be Jamie clowning around and making us laugh.

But the more my mother went back and forth to Jamie's and the more cars that came and went, the more I began to know that it wasn't a dream. No matter what we wished, or hoped, it was real.

In my room I dressed and I stared out my window. I saw my father come home, and I saw a long black limousine stop in front of Jamie's. I had seen these funeral cars before. Jamie and I had even talked about how we'd like to be rich enough to have one. We never thought about how they carried people to funerals. Especially we never thought of how one would carry people to Jamie's funeral.

As the cars pulled away, my father called. I knew they had been watching from downstairs.

"Where is Martha?" I asked as we walked to the car.

"Honey, she's too young. She doesn't understand what's going on."

I almost said, "Yes, she does," but I kept my mouth shut and got in the backseat with my sister. I thought about Martha with her short brown hair and her round face and no big brother. She didn't understand enough to cry, maybe that's what they meant. Or maybe she didn't understand about funerals. Well, I didn't understand either.

I could hear Martha's baby voice saying "heaben." Heaven was supposed to be such a wonderful place. I thought Jamie would be happier on the ground, playing with me and picking blackberries. It didn't seem possible for heaven to be so wonderful that you weren't even lonesome for the people and the things you knew before.

I wished Jamie could tell me. I closed my eyes and concentrated on listening to him. All I heard was the tires humming along the pavement.

I remembered when Jamie and I first learned that the earth revolved. We had plastered ourselves to the ground, with our arms stretched wide trying to feel the movement. Now I put one arm across my middle and pretended the rest of me was out straight, stiff. I couldn't make myself feel dead any more than I could feel the world spinning.

When we got out of the car my legs carried me along just out of habit. Clunk, clunk, clunk, up the sidewalk, up the steps, through the doorway.

The funeral parlor chapel was just like a church. Some of Jamie's and my friends were sitting together near the front. Mother nodded toward my friends. I couldn't tell who was who from the backs of their heads, except Heather. She had such golden hair, rather gold with a drop of red food coloring.

I looked up at Mom and Dad. I wanted to stay with them rather than sit with my friends, but I couldn't make the words come out. For a guy with a big mouth I sure was having trouble with words lately. I nodded to Mom and walked toward the front and sat down by Heather.

Maybe Heather would need me. I wouldn't cry. If I cried Heather was sure to start, and when Heather cried she bellowed. We looked at each other and spoke with our eyes, not talking, not smiling.

I wondered what she was thinking. Heather and Jamie and I, well, we'd been special to each other. Even though Jamie and I didn't like it that Heather was a girl.

And Heather and I talked about what a show-off Jamie was.

My eyebrows arched in surprise. Never until this very minute had I wondered what the two of them might have said about me.

Strains of music floated up from the organ. I looked around quickly. The casket had pale blue flowers on top. They looked like those big round chrysanthemums, but I had never seen any blue ones before. I didn't see Jamie's family anywhere.

A man got up and started talking and reading the Bible. He had some blue stripes in his tie that exactly matched the flowers on top of the casket. The matching blues held my attention over the droning of his words.

Flowers were everywhere. It made me think of Mrs. Mullins. She must be here somewhere, and she would know every one of these flowers. But this was more flowers than I'd ever seen before, even in Mrs. Mullins' garden.

I began studying every flower to brace myself against time. I remembered Uncle Jonah's funeral. It seemed like it had gone on forever. There was a quiet shift around me. Everyone was standing. Their standing pulled me up too, like reverse gravity.

In the car we waited for the procession to begin moving. A side door opened and Jamie's mother and father came out. They weren't leaning on each other; they were holding themselves very straight. I wanted to run to them and say something to them, but I was finding out that some things were impossible. Like making Jamie come back alive. I was almost choking in my throat.

I had automatically scrambled into the backseat with my sister, but now I wished I was snuggled in the front between my mother and my father. I swung one leg up and over the back of the front seat and flipped over and down.

This was strictly taboo. I'd heard "No climbing around in the car" almost as much as I'd heard about closing the door quietly. This time nobody said anything.

My mother put her arm around me from one side and my father from the other. It felt good.

The cemetery surprised me. We had passed it lots of times, but I had never paid much attention unless we were thinking about ghosts. So many people dead. I didn't know anyone dead except Uncle Jonah, and Jamie.

We turned off the paved road into the cemetery. We bumped gently down the rows between the graves. Things were green and pretty.

There was the hole. Jamie's hole. It was oblong and nice and even around the edges. If Jamie were here he would nudge me and say, "Look at that neat hole!" We had dug foxholes up in the woods but never could get them as squared off as he wanted.

The man with the blue stripes in his tie stood near the grave with his Bible and said some more things. I wasn't paying much attention. I was busy trying to make Jamie hear me, make him know I was there.

During the prayer I looked at the toes of my shoes. It was hard to think about God when something as small as a bee could kill your best friend.

Chapter 8

At supper I no longer felt it was disloyal to eat. If a miracle could have brought Jamie back, it would have been done already.

I was surprised, though, at how good everything tasted. I had heard it was like having cotton in your mouth, to eat when you were upset. But this tasted like cubed steak with gravy, all hot and delicious. I tried to make myself eat slowly, but my stomach kept urging me to grab everything in sight and stuff it down.

"That's okay," my father said. "Eat up." It made me smile to see that he had read my mind. I tried to swallow the smile.

"It's okay to smile, too," my dad said.

"Jamie would want you to do both." Well, that sure was the truth. Jamie would be the last one to want me to go around sad and starving. I ate three servings of everything.

I was tired and full and I went to sleep quickly. I didn't even kneel at the window and think about how Jamie wouldn't be sending me signals anymore.

But in the morning the first thing I saw was Jamie's house. It looked just exactly as it had a hundred other times. Even so, loneliness hung over it. Martha wasn't big enough to go popping in and out the doors all the time like Jamie and I did. And the baby, all he did was eat and sleep and lie there and smile.

Suddenly I thought about blackberries. They'd be ripe now. It seemed important to pick blackberries. I went downstairs and Mom poured milk over my cereal.

"I can put blackberries on my cereal tomorrow," I told her. I ate in such a hurry that milk sloshed on my chin, something it rarely did anymore. I rummaged under the sink and brought out two peck baskets.

"Two baskets," said Mother. "You really mean to pick a lot of berries, don't you?"

"One's for Jamie's mother," I said. I made a big thing of closing the door softly, and I grinned back at my mother.

I ran across to the road that dead-ended into the woods. I wished I was invisible. I didn't want anyone to see me, even Heather. I wanted to go blackberry picking with Jamie.

I hunched and picked my way into the thickest place. The stickers pulled at my sleeves and my socks. The berries were hanging so black and heavy that some of them fell into my hand at the merest touch. My mouth watered at the sight of the fat berries.

But Jamie and I had made a rule. No eating berries until we finished picking. Before we had made the rule, we used to eat as much as we picked. When we were through picking our baskets were still empty.

It seemed a long time since Jamie and I had snickered while the kids talked about us from the outside edge of the thicket. Was it just the other day? My throat felt funny when I thought of Jamie laughing so hard.

Every once in a while I pricked my thumb or fingers. I winced and put the hurt place to my mouth for comfort. Getting stuck was a part of berry picking.

The berries were ripening fast. I picked every fully black one. Some still had red places on them. Only a few were still all red, and none were green. I'd have to come picking every day, now, to catch them as

they ripened. I carried on a running con-
versation with myself, the berries, and
sometimes with Jamie.

Just you wait a minute, I'll pick you next.
There now, right into the basket with all
your friends.

Boy, look at those big ones, Jamie. I'll
take your mother the best ones.

Steadily, steadily my baskets filled. My
fingers were stained red-violet. I could smell
bubbling blackberry pie already. I bal-
anced berries one on another up and over
the top until I was afraid I couldn't carry
the baskets without spilling.

Then I took one plump berry between
my thumb and forefinger. It was so full-
to-popping that juice eased out onto my
finger. I let the berry stay on my tongue a
moment before I pressed it to the roof of
my mouth and let the juice trickle down
my throat.

Do you remember, I asked Jamie in my mind, the taste of blackberries?

I heard some of the gang playing as I walked back down the road. I wished myself invisible again. Heather's red-gold hair was swirling around her head. They were all up the hill, away from Jamie's. I needn't have worried about them seeing me. They were busy playing sling statue.

Games, I thought. And Jamie just dead. I shook my head, ashamed that they could so easily forget. Ashamed, too, that my own feet seemed anxious to run and jump and play.

I put my basket down on Jamie's porch and used my free hand to ring the bell. I kept changing my balance from one foot to the other. I was trying to think up what I would say to whoever answered the door.

Martha opened the door.

"Mama," she called immediately.

I wasn't expecting this. I hadn't meant to disturb Jamie's mother. I opened my mouth to protest, but as usual lately, I couldn't make the important words come out. I took turns scraping my bottom lip with my top teeth and my top lip with my bottom teeth.

And there she was, Jamie's mother. I knew her face and voice next best to my own mother's. Jamie and I were always banging in and out, being called on to close the doors quietly. Jamie's mother would often add, "The baby's sleeping."

I could tell she'd been crying. Her eyes were pale, as though they had faded in the wash. She pushed the screen door back and reached out for me. She didn't notice I was holding anything. I was afraid she would squeeze the basket and get blackberry stain on her dress.

She didn't cry. She pulled me close and

held me tightly, then eased back with her arm around my shoulder.

"I'm so glad to see you," she said, almost smiling. "It's been days. Thanks for helping out with Martha."

I smiled. Her voice was still the same. My brain was swirling with all the things I wanted to say and couldn't. I thrust out the basket of berries. My mouth twisted all out of shape when I tried to speak.

"Jamie and I were going to pick blackberries," I said.

She took the basket from me with one hand. With the other she touched my cheek and leaned down and kissed me on the forehead.

"How nice," she said. "I'll bake a pie. And you be sure to come slam the door for me now and then."

Joy burst within me and I blinked the stinging out of my eyes. I knew she understood everything I wanted to tell her.

"I will," I said. "Every day." I smiled, then laughed. I snatched up my basket of berries and ran home. I plopped them on the kitchen table and ran out again.

"I'm going up the street to play," I called behind me.

In my relief I felt that Jamie, too, was glad the main sadness was over. I wondered how fast angels, or whatever he was now, could move.

"Race you," I called to him, and I ran up the hill.